A NOTE TO PARENTS

The museum nearest you may not be just around the corner—as the Sesame Street Museum is for Ernie and Bert—but there is probably one within reach. A visit to the museum can stimulate your child's intellectual curiosity and imagination, opening the way to the excitement of discovery. Children who visit museums regularly when they are very young will continue to enjoy what museums have to offer as they grow older.

Most museums today present carefully designed exhibits, some just to look at and some to actively involve the visitor. Many museums, especially science or children's museums, offer special classes and programs as well. Don't try to show your child everything in the museum at once. Most museums have more exhibits than can be absorbed in one visit.

Not all museums have the variety of exhibitions found in Sesame Street's. Our museum is a composite designed to introduce your child to the many possibilities of museums, not to represent a typical museum or to teach specific science information.

Any museum can be fascinating to a child. Don't worry that some exhibitions may seem too sophisticated. Children respond at their own level of comprehension; they are not intimidated by new knowledge. For the very young, everything is new and a wonder.

A Random House PICTUREBACK®

A VISIT TO THE

With thanks to Dr. Edward Atkins,
Director of Content, *3-2-1 Contact.*

On *Sesame Street,*
Maria is performed by Sonia Manzano.

Library of Congress Cataloging-in-Publication Data: Alexander, Liza. A visit to the Sesame Street museum. (A Random House pictureback) SUMMARY: Curious to see a moon rock, Bert, Ernie, and Grover go to the Sesame Street Museum, where they find all the marvels of art, science, and history that a museum can offer, from dinosaurs to Egyptian mummies. [1. Puppets—Fiction. 2. Museums—Fiction] I. Mathieu, Joseph, ill. II. Title. PZ7.A37735Vi 1987 [E] 87-1685 ISBN: 0-394-88715-8 (trade); 0-394-98715-2 (lib. bdg.)

Manufactured in the United States of America   16 17 18 19 20

SESAME STREET MUSEUM

SESAME STREET MUSEUM

by Liza Alexander • illustrated by Joe Mathieu

FEATURING JIM HENSON'S SESAME STREET MUPPETS

Random House / Children's Television Workshop

One hot summer night everyone was sitting on the steps of 123 Sesame Street. Maria's cousin Donna was strumming her guitar.

"Look at the beautiful full moon," said Maria.

Everyone looked up.

"I wonder what the moon is really like," said Bert.

"Well, come to the Sesame Street Museum and I'll show you," said Donna, who worked there. "We have a rock that came from the moon. The astronauts brought it back."

"A moon rock!" exclaimed Bert. "I can't wait to see that."

Ernie and Grover wanted to see it, too, so the three of them decided to visit the museum the next day.

In the morning Grover, Ernie, and Bert met Donna on the steps of the museum.

"Hi! I'm so glad you came," said Donna. "It's my job to take children on tours through the museum every day. We have so many exciting things that I want to show you."

"I thought museums just had pictures," said Ernie.

"Our museum has something for everyone," said Donna. "Art and science exhibits and exhibits about how people lived a long time ago."

"What about the moon rock?" asked Bert.

Donna laughed. "Don't worry, Bert. We'll see the moon rock. It's part of the space exhibit."

They all went inside. "Follow me!" said Donna, and she led them up the big marble stairs. There were paintings hanging on the staircase wall. Some of them looked familiar.

"Hey, that's my house!" said Ernie.

"Right," said Donna. "A neighborhood artist painted it. Our museum has shows of paintings by local artists."

But Bert wasn't listening. He had run ahead of them.

"Look! It's the moon rock!" he shouted.

A huge purple crystal glittered in a glass case.

Donna and the others caught up. "No, Bert," said Donna. "That's not the moon rock. That's an amethyst. It came from deep inside our own earth, and it's part of the museum's geology collection."

Down the hall Ernie stopped at an open door. "What's in here?" he asked.

"Oh, this is Dr. Burke's workroom. This is where she and the other scientists prepare exhibits," said Donna, inviting them in.

"Hello," said Dr. Burke. "Look. I've just about finished rebuilding this old pot. We found it buried in a vacant lot on Sesame Street. The Dutch settlers used it for cooking more than three hundred years ago. Are you going to the Old Sesame Street exhibit?"

"Yes. That's just where we're heading," said Donna.

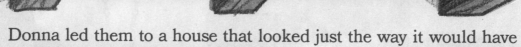

Donna led them to a house that looked just the way it would have looked three hundred years ago.

"Oh, Donna, this is terrific!" said Grover. "May we go inside, please?"

"Yes, that's what it's here for," she said.

Bert ran over to the butter churn and pretended that he was churning butter.

Grover rocked a wooden cradle. "Look at the cute little baby doll!"

Ernie tried on clothes like those the Dutch settlers had worn. "Hey, Bert, how do you like my hat?"

OLD SESAME STREET

After they had seen everything in the Old Sesame Street exhibit, Donna took Ernie, Bert, and Grover to the next hall. It was the Ancient Egyptian Room.

"Hey, Donna, do you have any mummies?" Ernie asked.

Donna smiled because children always asked about the mummies. She pointed to a beautifully painted mummy case standing in the corner, and Ernie and Grover ran over to it. But Bert had spotted something else. It was a big piece of stone.

"At last," he cried. "The moon rock!"

"I'm sorry to disappoint you, Bert, but that is a broken piece of monument," said Donna. "See all the little pictures on this side? That's ancient Egyptian writing called hieroglyphics."

When they left the Ancient Egyptian Room, Grover walked in a strange way down the hall.

"Look at me, everybody!" he said. "I am King Tut."

"Come on, Grover," said Bert. "Stop fooling around. We're here to see the moon rock!"

Ernie saw a water fountain. "Wait a minute," he said. "I need a drink of water. How about you, Bert?" asked Ernie, squirting water at Bert.

As they passed the prehistoric exhibit in the hall, Ernie stopped them.

"Look! What are those people doing cooking right here in the middle of the museum?" asked Ernie.

Donna laughed. "They aren't real people. They're dummies of cave people. This exhibit shows how prehistoric people lived thousands of years ago."

"Oh, my goodness. They had very big feet!" said Grover, looking down at his own small feet standing in two huge footprints.

"Grover, you are standing in dinosaur tracks," said Donna.

"Dinosaurs! Do you have them here too?" asked Bert, suddenly interested in something besides the moon rock.

"Sure," said Donna. "Follow the tracks."

Grover followed the dinosaur tracks into the next room, and the others followed Grover.

"*Yikes!*" cried Bert. "These are the biggest bones I've ever seen!"

"That is the skeleton of an *Apatosaurus*. He was a pretty big fellow," said Donna. "But not all dinosaurs were big. Take a look at those pictures of all kinds of dinosaurs."

And that is just what they did. They looked and looked. Even Bert forgot about the moon rock as he imagined what the earth was like millions of years ago.

APATOSAURUS

Next Donna took them to the children's workshop to see the experiments.

"Hey, look!" said Ernie. "There's Big Bird. What are you doing here, Big Bird?"

"I'm looking at one of my feathers through a microscope," Big Bird answered. "It makes things look much, much bigger! Here, Grover, take a look."

Grover looked through the microscope. "Oh, my goodness! That is a feather?"

Bert wanted to look too. "I didn't know museums had things you could *do*!" he said.

"Yes, Bert," answered Donna. "Most museums have Saturday morning or after-school programs for children. You can see some of the things kids do here at the Sesame Street Museum."

Near the window a boy was watering his plant in a tray of sprouting beans.

Nearby a girl was making a picture on a computer screen.

"The programs for children are different at every museum," said Donna. "Some even take children to the country on field trips to dig for fossils."

As they left the workshop and headed for the ocean exhibit, Donna explained how easy it is to join the children's program, just like Big Bird had.

The first thing they saw in the Ocean Hall was a gigantic great white shark hanging from the ceiling.

"Wow!" said Ernie. "Look at those teeth."

Around the room were many colorful fish and plants that live in the ocean.

"Gee, Donna," said Bert. "These fish are interesting, but aren't we ever going to see the moon rock?"

"Okay, Bert," she answered. "Right now!"

When they entered the space exhibit, Bert did not stop to look at the model of the solar system. He did not stop to look at the real astronaut's suit. He did not even look at the huge photograph of the first astronauts walking on the moon. Bert ran straight to a glass case standing in a spotlight in the middle of the room.

MOON ROCK

"The moon rock!" cried Bert happily.
Ernie caught up with Bert. "It looks just like any other rock," he said.
"Yes, but this rock came all the way from the moon! I think it is beautiful," sighed Bert dreamily.

Finally it was time to go home. On the way out, Donna took them to the museum shop where they could buy postcards, posters, models, and books about many of the exciting things they had seen in the museum.

Grover chose a book about an Egyptian king, and Ernie bought a tiny model of a dinosaur. Bert found a poster of the astronauts and a postcard of the moon rock to send to his cousin Bart.

In the lobby everyone said good-bye to Donna.

"That was terrific," said Grover. "Thank you for showing us everything in the museum."

Donna smiled. "Oh, there's a lot more to see. A museum's not a place you can see in just one visit."

"You mean we can come back tomorrow?" asked Bert.

"Yes, and as many times as you want," said Donna. And they did!

EXHIBITS

INFORMATION